GRAY
SKIES
TOMORROW

Gray
Skies
Tomorrow

A NOVEL

by

Silvia Molina

*Translated by John Mitchell and
Ruth Mitchell de Aguilar*

Plover Press
Kaneohe, Hawaii
1993

Grateful acknowledgment is hereby made for use of poetic epigraphs from
El otoño recorre las islas by José Carlos Becerra, 1973

Printed and bound in the United States of America

Design by Paula Newcomb
Cover illustration by Mirta Toledo

Library of Congress Cataloging-in-Publication Data

Molina, Silvia, 1946–
[Mañana debe seguir gris. English]
Gray skies tomorrow / by Silvia Molina ; translated by John Mitchell
and Ruth Mitchell de Aguilar.
p.   cm.
ISBN 0-917635-14-0 : $17.95. — ISBN 0-917635-15-9 (pbk.) : $8.95
I. Title.
PQ7298.23.05M313   1993
863—dc20   92-42497
CIP

Distributed by The Talman Company, Inc.
131 Spring St., New York, NY 10012

PQ
7298.23
.05
m313
1993

*To Elena Poniatowska, Hugo Hiriart
and Claudio*

Woman, woman,
watching me, did you see something, did you think you could
   see something?
Some little sign? Did you see it, did you see it?
Woman, "wayward child," "beautiful girl with no freedom,"
   shopworn phrases.
With me did you feel like the "wayward child," the
   "beautiful girl with no freedom"?
Contriving the torture, feigning the torture, were you
   torturing yourself more?
Did you feel like the pallid kid who walked at my side making
   faces, to whom I didn't speak?
Who did you think you were? Who did I think I was?

from La bella durmiente

José Carlos Becerra

1969

10 November

    I meet José Carlos Becerra.

    Rome: A demonstration in favor of divorce, organized by the "Italian League for Divorce," takes place here today. The demonstrators march peacefully with placards in front of the Chamber of Deputies.

11 November

    Supper at José Carlos's house.

    He almost keeps me there by force. He's a poet.

    Saigon: Today North Vietnamese troops attack a North American artillery base.

14 November

    I take a walk through London, accompanied by my friends.

    Mexico: Elenita Subirats beats Cecilia Rosado in straight sets: 6–2, 6–2.

17 November

    My friends abandon us. (Me and London.)

    Prague: Czechoslovakian students remember victims of Nazi repression and pay homage at the tomb of Jan Palach, who burned himself to death to protest the Soviet occupation.

18 November

    I realize that staying at my aunt's apartment won't be completely agreeable. Besides, I won't be able to sleep on the sofa. But I'll have to get used to it. (To my aunt and the sofa.)

Madrid: Five foreigners are detained, having been accused of possessing and distributing pornographic books and pictures.

21 November
My nearest relative watches me constantly.
London: The *Daily Telegraph* says today that the Brazilian government is trying to silence the opposition of Dominicans and students by means of torture and jail.
Apollo 12 returns to the moon.

22 November
I visit the home of Charles Dickens with José Carlos. I like him, I like him a lot. (José Carlos, of course.)
Dallas, Texas: Six years have passed since Kennedy's assassination.

23 November
I hope he calls me soon.
France: De Gaulle fails to celebrate his birthday today.

29 November
We tour Tate Gallery together. Yes, I believe it's true: I'm in love.
London: In this city there is a foreigner who is in love with a poet!

1, 2, 3, 4, 5, 6, 7, 8, 9, 10, 11, 12 December
We are seeing each other secretly, and I have so many problems that I don't have time to see what's going on in the world.

13 December

He offers me nothing, but after all, what can I offer him?

London: John Lennon and his wife protest the English attitude toward the war between Biafra and Nigeria.

14 December

I am going to José Carlos's apartment, ready for any and all . . . I return very cast down.

17 December

I am the happiest woman in the world!

18 December

I am going to see a doctor. I am very apprehensive. *Later*: I'm reassured.

Paris: Blackout for a few hours.

19 December

It's incredible! I love José Carlos and I'm going to Windsor with an Englishman. How can I let myself be trapped this way?

20 December

We celebrate Joseph and Mary's search for lodging. San Sebastian, Spain: The Basque provinces are shaken by a metalworkers' strike. Now ten thousand workers are out in a show of solidarity.

21 December

I read in one of the city's dailies that Jacqueline Onassis arrives elegantly dressed in London to spend the Christmas holidays. Where will I spend them and how?

25 December
    Today is Christmas and there is nothing that will
    make me accept it as such.

26 December
    For me today is Christmas: I am with José Carlos.
    Washington: Agents of the U.S. Information Agency
    ask the Soviet Union to end its radio interference
    with Russian language broadcasts of the *Voice of
    America*.

29 December
    José Carlos always cooks when we're together and
    does it very well.
    Paris: José Fores, the Spanish refugee who was given
    a heart transplant the twenty-fourth of November,
    1968, dies today.

31 December
    I don't know how these things happen, but we eat at
    Hugo and Lucinda's house.

I copy these lines from *Relación de los hechos*:
    We deliver ourselves for an instant to the *instant*;
    for a moment we cease to exist in all the places
        where we are remembered or forgotten;
    the laws of the city don't touch us;
    for an instant we are *the others*,
    those two about whom we dream so much.

1970

1 January

José Carlos hides my purse to make me stay with him. I want to stay with him, but what about later? El Salvador: There is an epidemic of dysentery.

2 January

He gives me the key to his apartment. To vary the routine, I don't go to school.

3 January

I take his clothes to the laundry while he writes.

4 January

Marlo likes me and Cristina doesn't know it. Mexico: The movie *Krakatoa, East of Java* has been at the theater *Diana* for sixteen weeks.

6 January

If I could tell Cristina the truth about Marlo . . . Sao Paulo: The betrothal of Manuel Bezerra, Catholic priest, to 18-year-old Deise Jamarco is the event of the year.

7 January

I am firmly resolved to go to school tomorrow. Tokyo: The former Japanese ambassador Ichiro Kawasaki, who was removed from his post for writing a book critical of his country, returns to Argentina, but this time as director of a Japanese soccer team.

8 January

> We go to the movies. At times he's less than nice to me, but he says it's because he loves me.
> Edinburgh, Scotland: It is the opinion of Dr. Manning that it would be worthwhile to offer a reward of twelve hundred dollars to persons who agree to be sterilized.

9 January

> Yes, today I'm on my way to school.

10 January

> We explore every corner of London.

11 January

> José Carlos wants me to decide to live with him.
> Mexico: Important up-and-coming business seeks secretary with the following qualities: No more than 25 years old. Good appearance and manner. Takes dictation rapidly. Command of the English language.

16 January

> I take the pill regularly.
> Moscow: Happy Moldavia with its exquisite wines presents a problem for the Kremlin, which watches sadly as that small Soviet republic works little and drinks a lot.

17 January

> I'm going to look for work. It's urgent.
> Boston: The Kobeirskis are declared out of danger. An operation to separate the Siamese twins was performed November 25.

18 January
    I have a friend. Her name is Patricia.
    Mexico: Manuel Martínez displays his skill with the
    cape.

22 January
    I would like to write a book although he might not
    read it.
    Santiago de Chile: The Marxist leader Salvador
    Allende is put forward as a candidate for President of
    the Republic.

23 January
    José Carlos cooks delicious food.
    London: Seven out of ten in England say that the
    maxi-skirt is not practical (without defining exactly
    what is meant by "practical").

25 January
    I am under the influence of a drug. I don't know
    what it is.
    Johannesburg, South Africa: A cake costing 12,500
    pesos and weighing 220 pounds is made for the wed-
    ding of the famous Dr. Christian Barnard and Barbara
    Zoeller.

29 January
    My days are spent in constant war with myself and
    always I reply that I love him.
    Badajoz, Spain: The tallest man in the world, Gabriel
    Eslovomenjai (8½ feet in height and 440 pounds in
    weight), arrives in this city to submit to a thorough
    medical examination.

3 February
> José Carlos begins planning his trip through Europe.
> To think that I have less than fifty dollars!
> Wales: Bertrand Russel dies at age 97.

5 February
> We talk endlessly. I almost live in his apartment. I
> promise him that I will try to meet him in Bilbao,
> but I think it will be difficult.

12 February
> He has many problems with English and says that he
> is going to make me his official interpreter. Since I
> never go to school, who will be mine?
> London: Prince Philip goes to Mexico.

13 February
> Cristina is very much in love with Marlo. If only she
> knew . . .

14 February
> I don't know how it's possible that José Carlos knows
> so much about everything.

17 February
> I can't stop thinking that soon you will go away.
> Mexico: An Aztec religious offering is found in the
> subway's Pino-Suárez station.

18 February
> There are chances for work.
> New Orleans: Aspirin is labeled a contaminant.

20 February
> I will live with Patricia.
> Mexico: Palafox is selected for the Davis Cup.

26 February
> I haven't seen him for days. Who could he possibly
> be going out with?
> London: John Lennon says it's Picasso's turn to be
> mobbed at one of his art expositions.

7 March
> I am a Spanish teacher.
> Oaxaca, Mexico: Multitudes watch the solar eclipse.

9 March
> He loves me, of that I am sure.

11 March
> I take a walk in the woods with Marlo. I don't know
> what I'm going to tell Cristina.

12 March
> It's inevitable. Soon he'll go. I don't know what's
> going to become of me during that time.

16 March
> Shut up all day long. We make a pact: we will love
> each other all our lives!

24 March
> He insists that I catch up with him. He gives me the
> names of the places where he will wait for me.
> Leave-taking.

25 March

He leaves London.
Desolation . . .

31 March

You wait for me in Bilbao, but I don't arrive. Day
after day I consult the map, following your footsteps.

11 April

Already there's not much point in writing all this.
Where are you at this moment?
London: The Beatles announce their separation.
General consternation.

21 April

Fortunately I'm occupied with classes.
London: The British government will print stamps
with the likeness of various characters from Dickens
as part of the first centennial of the author's death.

3 May

My days pass slowly. I go from my apartment to
Patricia's to drop off some of my clothes, from there
to school, and after classes I always invent some
chore.
Santiago de Chile: A bicephalous baby dies within
fifteen minutes of being born.

16 May

I write my mother that I am moving.
Cairo, Egypt: Difficulties continue with Israel.

27 May

Brindisi, Italy: The Mexican poet José Carlos
Becerra—born in Villahermosa, Tabasco, in the year

1937—, dies today in an automobile accident—at the age of thirty-three—, in the vicinity of San Vito de Normanni. He was driving a secondhand car in which he took a curve at high speed, losing control of the automobile, which broke the safety rail and fell into a gorge at the edge of the sea. He died instantly of a fracture at the base of the skull.

GRAY
SKIES
TOMORROW

1

*You can pretend you are pretending, you can counterfeit
    that you are you,
that your desire and not your amnesia is your true
    accomplice, that your amnesia is the guest you
    poisoned
the night they ate together.
You can say what you want; that will be the truth,
although neither you nor they can ever prove it.*

It's November. We turn up the collars of our overcoats,
fix our glances downward, and while we walk our feet
make a strange medley on the sidewalk. "I told you we
should have bought some boots." Paddington Station has
been left behind; when we ask an aged news vendor,
"*Queensway? Please!*" he points with his finger straight
ahead.

I arrive at the apartment with my two friends. A swarthy
woman with a broad forehead opens the door, and her
large, brilliant eyes declare her friendliness.

"Come in, come in. We've been waiting for you. You
didn't get lost?"

"Hi, there!"

"Nice to know you."

"Welcome!"

We leave our overcoats on the coat rack in the entrance,
which reminds me in some way of my grandmother's
house in Mexico. I know that from this day forward I will
see every kind of coat rack in London. We cross through
a little corridor toward the parlor, and as we pass near the
kitchen my companions sigh. I also think how our stom-

achs have been sacrificed in the course of our trip and savor the idea of eating soon, as they do. One of my friends takes the lead.

"This is Hugo Gutiérrez Vega," she tells us.

"How are you?"

"Good afternoon."

A young man with a childlike expression on his face gets up from his seat. Hugo makes a gesture for us to sit down at the same time that he introduces him. It is José Carlos Becerra, and as he shakes his head to remove a lock of hair that is falling across his forehead he gives us a very frank smile.

"What would you like to drink?"

"Sherry, please."

"How long have you been here? What are your plans?"

"We only called you last night, but we've already been here three days. We have been sightseeing, you know. Unfortunately we have to leave for Mexico, but she stays," says one of my friends, referring to me.

"You'll like it. This is the perfect city to live in. You'll see."

"That's the reason I wanted her to meet you," my friend adds.

Then José Carlos turns to me:

"What a coincidence. I've only been here a short while and was also told to look up Hugo. They're great people. Once you come here, you can't escape. You always return. Where are you going to live?"

"At my aunt's house. You must know her. There can't be that many Mexicans who work here."

"You've already moved in?"

"No, she doesn't know I've arrived yet. I'm going to show up Monday, after my friends leave. I don't know what excuse I'll give."

Our conversation carries us through Europe, our adventures, Hugo's work, politics in Mexico, the activities of my aunt, English customs, our difficulty in understanding the language, until Lucinda, Hugo's wife, indicates it's time for dinner.

The dining room forms part of the parlor in which we are sitting. There are bookcases everywhere. They seat me opposite José Carlos. Twice, perhaps, I take my eyes from him: he doesn't look at his plate. I don't understand how he can watch me, eat, and participate with such enthusiasm in the table conversation.

Outside, I don't know when, it has stopped snowing; and I wonder if I like those drops which begin to fall. I try to go across the room to have coffee with the rest, but José Carlos is quizzing me and we sit down again at the table, just the two of us, near the window, in order to feel closer to the rain.

"What are you planning to do here?"

"First, to study English. And you?"

"I have a scholarship."

"To do what?"

"To travel, I am going to travel."

"I don't believe that. Who gave you the scholarship?"

He tells me about his life. He's a poet, desirous of remaining in London some time. He admires the English writers, some of whom he feels have greatly influenced him. He describes his early years in the tropics—"You're from Villahermosa? You know, I was born in Campeche. You like cashew nuts?" His world as a student in Mexico City—"What's it like to live in a boarding house?" His work—"Remember, I'm holding you to that book." What he's doing and what he's living for: he says he wishes to travel, to know the world and the cradle of civilization, to live, to have new experiences so that he can continue writing. I speak to him about my anthropology studies, of the pleasure I get from reading, of my intentions to write something (as we bring Kafka to the table with us) about Prague and its black doors and its tiered tombs. My friends begin to say goodbye: José Carlos gives us his address and invites us to his apartment the next evening.

We thank our host and hostess: a splendid meal, and when we say goodbye they say we're always welcome.

2

At the climax, the last phrase, one
of the two (we two) raised a shield defensively.
The other launched his blow blindly.

Oxford Street, shops, shops, and more shops. "But if you've already bought six sweaters, we should get going, shouldn't we? And you, it looks as if you're planning to sell Hindu silk handkerchiefs in Mexico." I am worn out, but my friends want to buy everything, having saved their money to leave it here and depart the city with only enough to tip the porter at the airport. I buy some lined gloves and return to the hotel, buried under a large quantity of my friends' bundles.

We're tired, we each take a bath, and all get ready to go to José Carlos's house. One tries on a new dress, another curls her hair. I'm sleepy, I'm tired of carrying their things from one place to another, and I'd like to go to bed. Although I think I can see him anytime, they encourage me: these are our last days together and we have to make the most of them.

"You better hurry, little girl. We don't want to be late."

The subway station where we arrive is on London's outskirts, suburbs that look like little towns within the larger city. "Are you sure he lives around here? Mightn't we be lost?" We pass near a public park and see various people walking their dogs before going to bed. Everywhere the buildings look the same. We stop at a group of them that share a small enclosed garden at the front. "Yes, I think this is it." I feel unusually agitated inside.

José Carlos opens the door and gives us all a kiss. He

introduces another Mexican who works for the BBC and has his arms around a severe, somewhat common girl whom we greet courteously. If José Carlos had kissed only me, I would have sworn that he squeezed my hand softly. Could he have greeted the others in the same way? "It's good for driving away the cold," José Carlos tells us, referring to the wine that he serves in some tumblers, before going to hang up our coats. Time passes and suddenly the English girl says something to José Carlos's friend that we don't understand; she has been sitting for hours without being able to laugh, smiling artificially, when she sees something in our faces, perhaps in reply to her companion's scarce translations. José Carlos goes out to say goodbye to them, and we sit on the floor, waiting, not far from the fire in the little fireplace. When he returns, he lies down full length on the hardwood planking, places his head on my thighs, and again squeezes my hand lightly. I turn questioningly to look at one of my friends, who turns coldly away and exchanges a mocking look with the other. I know that the warmth I am feeling is not from the fire that is very near and that the color in my face is not natural, but somehow I like his daring. I have the desire to stroke his hair and to search out his hand.

A little later one of my friends looks at her watch:

"We're happy here, José Carlos," she says, looking at me, "but if we don't go we'll miss the last train."

"Yes, except that I'm sorry to tell you that I have decided to keep her with me," he replies, meanwhile taking me by the waist.

I separate myself brusquely. "What's the matter with you?"

"You're staying."

He disappears in search of the overcoats.

"You're already caught, little girl."

"Sh! Don't be foolish."

"Why pretend? He's keeping you!"

"Please, shh, don't be like that. I swear I'm more surprised than you are. I swear it."

"Sure, why not? Certainly."

He comes toward us with only two overcoats; I run into the room, take my coat from on top of his bed and, when I emerge from the doorway, my friends have already gone. We're alone and I feel a little afraid.

"Please, let me go; I know it's a joke. Waaait! Open the door."

"Stay."

"You're crazy."

"You're not staying?"

"Certainly not. Cuh-ming! Cuh-ming!"

"Shhh! You're going to wake the neighbors."

"Let me out."

"Give me a kiss."

He has his eyes closed. I search for a spot on his bearded cheek, although I know I'd like his mouth. I barely kiss him. He opens the door, and I go out like a shot in the direction of the elevator. Down in the street, I take the road that leads to the station. My friends are already at the entrance when I catch up to them.

"You're stupid! You should have stayed."

"What a fool, what a fool!" one of them adds. "Me, they don't have to ask twice."

"But with me they do."

3

Destiny. Word that the bottom of the river pulls out like
  a fish,
like a cheek where the current is able to weep
without the banks noticing it.

The Tower of London, Saint James, a photograph in Buck-
ingham Palace, stunned by Westminster, we go on to Par-
liament, admire Big Ben, London Bridge, more shopping,
the pubs, more photographs and goodbye.

"Oh, you, but we're not going to die; no need for such
a long face."

"Write us soon. Stay close to Hugo. With them you
won't feel so lonely."

"If I were you, I'd look up his friend. Don't pretend
you don't like him."

"Look alive, little girl," she says, referring to José Carlos,
"and don't put on that face of 'it wasn't me, it was Ester.'
Look alive, my girl. Look a-live!"

The days my friends remained here are over like the
wink of an eye, their departure the saddest, and from Vic-
toria Station I call my aunt, announcing my arrival.

The driver stops in front of the building. The taxi is one
of the elegant sort that they have here: black, roomy, and
well-cared for. A slender gentleman in a gray suit opens
the door so that I can get out. Of all that he says, I understand only: "Please, miss." He's helpful, letting me know
by his glance that he expects me. He takes my baggage
agilely, in spite of his advanced age, which is accentuated
by his white hair, and conducts me in silence to the third
floor.

"How scandalous! Such an hour to arrive! They're waiting for me at the office."

You're crazy; you're not going to be able to stand her. If you don't like it, you're going to have to stay anyway because I'll not send you a return ticket; a trip like this costs a lot and this is not a game we're playing . Think about it carefully. Better to change your mind now, because remember, she can be rather difficult.

My companion in the gray suit sets down the suitcases and makes a sign, indicating he is going to withdraw. I thank him; my aunt introduces me; then Mr. Wolpert disappears down the hall.

"Don't sit in that armchair, you'll get it dirty. Don't unpack anything until I get back and tell you where to put your clothes. You can take a bath to relax and heat up something to eat."

My eyes and the door close at the same time. I make up an age for José Carlos: about thirty-two. I like his moustache. One of my friends bought herself a pretty skirt, the other is going to see her boy friend and maybe get married. Poor thing, she lost her camera in Paris.

Following my arrival and in the days that follow, my aunt is friendlier towards me. I have nothing special to do and help her with everything. I go to her office and remain there while she works. I accompany her on shopping trips; she takes me to some places of interest; we eat at one or another prestigious restaurant; we visit the pubs; I begin to understand how the city works. Now I'm able to go by myself to the subway station and the bus without getting lost, and I decide to go to the school. The *International House* is in Soho, two blocks from Piccadilly, where I see everything: the small Italian restaurant as well as the one serving Hindu food, the large theater, bargain basements, hippies . . . I go there to spend a little of my time every day, and I attend classes happily.

I am a little more independent, but my aunt watches my every step: she invites me to dinner every day and entrusts me with annoying little errands that I continue running for fear of her scenes, her anger. I'm sure that today it will fall to my lot to search for the umbrella she left at the beauty salon and "in passing ask the grocer if I left my glasses case there yesterday." Of course, I will also have to use the dictionary to look up any new word she drops "so that you can continue increasing your vocabulary."

4

Come here with your collection of butterflies, with your
old toys that no longer exist
and that seem to mock you from various corners;
come here with your traces of the astonished child.

The telephone rings. Out of sorts, thinking that surely my aunt has forgotten something, I go to answer.

"What number is this?"

"Yes, José Carlos?"

"I invite you to visit the home of Dickens tomorrow."

"Who gave you my telephone number?"

"Do you want to go?"

"What fun! It's a wonderful idea."

"I'll come by for you at ten in the morning."

I have waited for my aunt fairly anxiously. I tell her I met him in school and give him a thousand qualities so that she won't have any objections.

"You're not going."

"But why not? After my mother allowed me to travel alone through Europe, now you prohibit me from visiting a museum?"

"But here you are my responsibility."

"I'm going to go."

"You are a thankless child; I feel sick. I am ill, and instead of keeping me company you go out with a perfect stranger. I need some medicine from the pharmacy and . . ."

"I'll go right away for your medicine and, by the way, I am going out."

José Carlos has come for me. My aunt enters the parlor in her dressing gown to meet him.

"I told this girl that she shows a lack of concern by leaving me alone, because I am feeling very ill," is her salutation to José Carlos, who remains silent.

I feel again that the color in my face is not my own, and I can't think of anything to speed our exit beyond saying goodbye. I try to give my aunt a kiss, but she remains immobile, looking at José Carlos as if she'd like to take him to pieces. We enter the elevator without saying anything. I don't know what to say or do. I still feel embarrassed.

"How do you endure that harpy?" he asks me, on reaching the street.

I don't answer, allowing myself to be lured toward him. We walk arm in arm while he speaks again of his restlessness, asks me the names of the trees, imitates the song of birds. I'm learning more about him: his curiosity about everything.

Already we're in Dickens' house: José Carlos pours out his feelings about each object, each picture, each stair tread; and he speaks of everything as if he's been here before, as if Dickens and his characters were his brothers.

A group of tourists with a guide at their head comes near us and we fall in with them. I try the best I'm able to translate for José Carlos, all the words of the man conducting us through the rooms, and discover to my astonishment that José Carlos has told me all that and more.

While we eat in a pub near Hugo and Lucinda's house, I feel again how his look goes right through me, and I'm disturbed. He remarks on the friendship he feels for Hugo, and we decide to stop by for a visit. I no longer feel like a stranger with them, but enter smoothly into the conversation as if it were José Carlos who has involved me. Nightfall makes me remember my aunt and I ask to return home alone. There is no reason to interrupt such an agreeable social occasion, so distant from the rain and reproaches of my aunt, "who must have been waiting for me such a long time."

Reaching the apartment, I sense trouble. The light in the parlor, which by night serves as my bedroom, is lit, and Mr. Wolpert warns me in a low voice:

"Take care. She's in a bad mood."

I feel the desire to ask him to come with me to the door, to clasp me to him. I expect a scene, "a little number," and I can't help being afraid. One, two . . . nor do I even have a key; I need to get one . . . three and I knock.

"Don't tell me that all day you've been at Dickens' house. He's too old, unkempt, and bearded for you."

One, two, three, four, five, six, seven, ei . . .

"Where did you go?"

"To Dickens' house."

"And after? Or did you spend twelve hours at Dickens' house?"

"To eat."

"And then? Or did you spend ten hours eating?"

"To the house of some friends of his."

"And do you expect me to believe you? Aren't there any telephones?"

Eight, nine, ten, eleven, twelve, thirteen . . .

5

But my love, I repeat, but the nature of my disguise,
  but my existence as rain,
suffered the eyedropper of the most sordid surprises,
  the most cowardly and beautiful,
and my afflictions and my well being, the debts of my
  blood and my last roses—
suffered and completed this chain that Reason and Law
  have lined with velvet and with Science.

A week has gone by with hardly a quarrel with my aunt. After school I'm prompt for meals, and I remain in the apartment the rest of the time. During the evenings I ask myself why it is that José Carlos hasn't called. I desire without succeeding to dream about him; I give free rein to my imagination; we go here and there together; also we have kissed many times.

This morning before I go out for school, the phone finally rings. He invites me to the Tate Gallery; we'll meet in the subway; he doesn't want to run into that monster of an aunt of mine again, as he has nicknamed her. I feel how my stomach begins to contract; I am dying to see him.

I meet my aunt, as is customary, at mealtime; I tell her that Saturday morning I am going out with José Carlos, and I hear the words which I now know by heart.

Dawn has come. I have waited I don't know how many hours for daylight. It hasn't stopped raining, my aunt bangs things around, and I visualize Mr. Wolpert whispering in my ear: *Take care.* I imagine that tall lady with severe features and cold looks, always redolent of perfume, is only an invention of the rain.

31

"When he comes for you, I'm going to tell him . . ."

"We agreed to meet in the subway."

"But . . . how is this possible? What sort of man is he that he won't even come to your house for you? Only those with bad intentions make dates in such places. You're not going."

"Don't make me see him on the sly."

"And my responsibility? I am going to write to your mother."

"My mother respects me and has confidence in me."

For the first time since I left my house, I miss her. A homesickness for my mother comes over me. I long to cry, but I mustn't give my aunt that pleasure.

I am tired of waiting for him. I have walked back and forth through the passageway many times. This place is now a bore for me, and I remain seated on a bench, asking myself in anguished tones if he will come. In the distance I spot him by his red muffler. I'm on my feet, watching as José Carlos approaches smiling, always the great observer. He reads my mood and loosens my hair; his eyes meet mine and we embrace.

"Break out of all this."

"I can't, without money . . ."

"She's a . . ."

"The thing is she has always lived alone this way and suddenly finds herself unable to share."

"A lie. She's guilty of moral blackmail, manages you, wishes to manipulate you. You don't leave because you don't want to."

José Carlos has completely altered while talking of my aunt; now I know his hatred also.

Suddenly we have changed the subject and I am laughing. When he speaks, certain letters are dragged out by his rather unusual accent, and I amuse myself imitating him.

He says that I am a child, and I reproach him by saying that only the other day I was a woman. He overwhelms me; we feel tempted to caress each other; on the way to the gallery a mutual desire is building. Besides, it's raining.

My knowledge of painting is, by the furthest stretch, rudimentary. I ask José Carlos how it is that, knowing so much about everything, he goes out with me, who know nothing. He says that my capacity . . . that together . . . and once more I am off on cloud nine.

He knows the majority of pictures from reproductions, and seeing the originals is like a banquet. We walk tirelessly, from picture to picture, from room to room, with senses wide open; in each one he points out the theme, the significant details, the technique, the period, and the feeling conveyed. He makes a poem of one painting and of the next says something that another poet has written. In this way he makes me feel that the acts of painting and writing are manifestly blessed.

On leaving the gallery, we go off in no fixed direction; we walk without knowing where. We eat something in a little cafe and two hours later find ourselves in the Bloomsbury neighborhood.

José Carlos pulls me to one side. Coming toward us is a tall thin woman with a long angular face and enormous shoes; she wears a black dress and her eyes are deep in their sockets. He squeezes my hand at the same time that he asks me if I have read her books. I don't know what he's referring to. On seeing that she's gone, he excuses himself:

"It was the Woolf," he jokes. "I was going to introduce her to you, but I preferred not to interrupt her because she appeared to be a little upset, and I was afraid she might fly into a rage or cry."

6

Yes, I am fleeing;
in my heart the night is disguised as a heart,
in my hair the wind is disguised as hair;
my face is so dark that the stars have flown my borders.

The British Museum, the National Gallery . . . we go out
without my aunt knowing it. Today we're at the movies
with Hugo and Lucinda. While we're watching the film,
José Carlos loosens my hair as though it were an old custom. On the way back to the Gutiérrez Vegas' house, I
decide I've lived this scene various times. During supper I
hear Bergman, Bogart, Fellini and Buñuel named contin-
ually. I'm unsure of myself and speak little. I never want
to leave here—it's so nice—but this time it's José Carlos
who urges that we go.

The bus stops for us and we climb to the uppermost
part, where we are the only passengers. He wants me to
come to his apartment and I justify my fears instinctively.
I say it's late, that my aunt must be expecting me. José
Carlos becomes irritated, talks roughly, hammers home his
words, almost shouts.

"I don't understand how you stand her."

"It's that she's the only one I have."

"No, you're a coward."

"My problem is mon . . ."

"Money isn't worth shit; come and live with me."

"Your scholarship hardly sees you through."

"Work. Look for a job."

"I'm a minor and . . ."

"Son of a bitch! It's all in yourself. If you wanted to,
there'd be no problem."

"I promise you I'll think . . ."

We arrive at my apartment and once more he begs me to accompany him to his—nor is it yours, I think, when the person who loaned it to you returns. We embrace; I only remember where I am when I hear someone coughing with discreet insistence. I open my eyes. Mr. Wolpert warns me with that look he is always using; in fact, it's repeated daily until I can no longer stand it.

Inside the building, I take the stairs. Stopping between the second and third floors, I sit down on a stair tread to think: what do I want to think about? About the movie we saw? No, there ought to be some way out of this. To talk with my aunt, no. Finding work? I close my eyes, strangling my desire to cry out. I relive the scene below, ignoring Mr. Wolpert. A little later I turn the key in the lock, trying not to make any noise, for I see no light.

"What an hour to get home."

"Good night."

"Who do you think you are?"

She goes on talking; I'm not interested in what she says. After washing the dishes I will go to bed. From what I can see, Esperanza didn't come today either. How come, Esperanza, how come? Don't tell me that you're thinking of not coming back to do the cleaning, with all the pleasure I get when you offer me tea and speak of a thousand things, of your daughter my age, that because you've worked so many years at the embassy you already feel like a Mexican. You always tell me that you come on the *q.t.*, and I beg you to keep on doing it. You'll come again, won't you? Yes? In short, tomorrow is another day; I will go to see Lucinda, to ask for her advice.

By chance I discover a letter addressed to me; it's from my mother. My aunt pigeon-holed it; surely she fears a plot. Within a few months I will reach my majority; then my allowance will no longer go to her. She's worried

36

because she needs that money. My brothers and sisters ask for me; I'm surprised. Sure, why not: "Dear brothers and sisters who miss me, here you've got me under the continuous drizzle of London, free of your ill usage. Ah, my older sister must miss my blouses, shirts, suits, and shoes a lot! Too bad you can't be here! I'll gladly loan every single thing, and if you want I'll also loan you my aunt, who fits me a little large. As for my brothers, I beg that if you really miss me, don't scratch my records, don't loan my books, and don't scare my friends. I want to ask you, now who do you annoy all day with your *go see, tell him, bring me, do me the favor, put this away, get rid of that*, etc., etc., etc.? I want to console you: here they bother me in your stead."

Mama has sent some money and in closing urges me to write more often, saying I can count on her for everything. While I sleep, I give that "everything" many forms.

7

Now this word:
when the breath of smoke and dust of the ailing city
    is lifted from parks on the west wind,
when the abandoned streets sit down to eat their own
    herbs like ancients in forgetfulness,
when the overstuffed evening streetcar stops at a corner
and only a sad girl gets off . . .

Now in the subway en route to school, I have made a decision. I accept the rules of the game. I double my bet and direct my steps to the apartment of José Carlos. In front of the door I can't seem to knock; I think that the best pretext is to have no pretext and that the only permissible doubt is whether you've succeeded in not doubting. And now, what do I say to him? That I've come because I wanted to see him, to feel his hands squeezing my waist, to hear that he has decided to keep me? "I have nothing to read and I thought that you might be able to loan me a book in Spanish because here it's so hard to get them . . ." No, better: "Mr. Wolpert noted a telephone call for me at the desk, and since they didn't leave their name I thought that it was you and came over." I knock, he comes out, I will not say anything. I'll let him be the one to begin and then . . . Is it possible to be someone capable of saying why she comes without subterfuges? I came here because I love you . . .

It's going to be easier than I imagined. José Carlos knows it; he will know it when he sees me. We won't say anything; he knows my expressions. José Carlos, are you going to help me? Some voices rise in the apartment in front; it

39

looks like the morning will go on being gray; I would return to the station, but it's necessary to cross the garden again and I'm already here. I close my eyes. The doors hold secrets and the walls are labrynthine. I find myself in one of the passageways; will it really be the exit? Outside, London is motionless; everything has stopped for me.

When I open my eyes, the woman in the apartment in front is looking at me, and for a moment I feel inclined to offer explanations: "Does my cousin live here? I'm making a survey. What do you think about the television series *Henry the Eighth and His Six Wives*?" Don't look at me that way, it's not what you think. Speak out, yes; that would be better than resisting those daggers, that reproach. You're dying to know what must go on inside here, right? Imagine the worst for you and the most beautiful for me, for us. Have you ever been in love? Mrs. Neighbor of José Carlos, Mrs. Family, Mrs. Society: this time, I am not going to explain.

I ring the bell. I have the sensation of stripping myself of something; I loosen my hair the way he likes; the rain blows sharply across the entrance; I get rid of my forlornness. Here I am. Nothing that is or has been part of my surroundings matters to me. I no longer dream a desire, I am a possibility. I see it, embody it, feel it. I am an act repeated through the centuries: the yielding.

He's not here. He's not here. HE'S NOT HERE. HE'S NOT HERE. He's not here! HE'S NOT HERE! Isn't he here? ISN'T HE HERE? He's not here. Come out. Come out, PLEASE. Come out from wherever you are. Come open this door. Come. Can he be sleeping? José Carlos, are you going to do this to me? OPEN, open, please.

"Are you still RINGING, young lady?"

" . . . "

" *STOP RINGING.*"

José Carlos, will I have the courage to gamble another

day? From here to the subway, from there to the school, from there to my aunt's apartment. To arrive at the station I must cross the garden again, like Napoleon abandoning Russia: beaten. The soldiers walk along shame-faced; they wish it were over once and for all and long for their hearths. And mine, where is it?

A friendly hand removes my finger which is still pressing the button. It's the neighbor. José Carlos is not in, she explains to me. I understand, but my face must remind her of someone from a lunatic asylum.

8

Thus I will hold something of yours in the world.
In this way each word will be marked forever.

I have come back. This time, yes. He is there, working at his typewriter. The keys sound like footsteps. I place my ear against the wall, where the sound is augmented: *tap, tap, tap,* continuous, rhythmical.

I press the doorbell softly.

9

Now your body knows what it is to be your body, what
it means for you to be him;
your body extended at the full length of your love, at the
full length of your soul, and all the boats that set sail
from your heart go now with lights extinguished.

I told Lucinda what happened and she has consented to
accompany me to the doctor's. For the first time since I
came here the weather is good. We get off the bus at Por-
tobello Road. I ask Lucinda what's the meaning of so many
people and all those hippies everywhere. It's like La Laguni-
illa, she explains. She warns me several times not to waste
time inquiring about pieces of silver, bronze, copper, porcelain, furniture, jewels, clothing. I touch everything without really seeing it, with the aim of delaying my encounter
with the physician: I have come because . . . I came to see
you for . . . look, doctor, it's that . . .

"Hurry, you can come here some other day; there are
always a lot of people at the clinic."

We stop at a gable-roofed house. A woman opens the
door; seated in silence, a young man and a girl wait their
turns. They don't speak; they don't look at us, giving an
impression of indifference about what goes on around
them. I can't rid myself of a feeling of guilt. Lucinda pushes
me toward the nurse's desk. There is a bench, but I can't
sit down. I have the feeling I'm in court.

"*What's your name?*"

"I've come because I believe it's the best thing to do."

"*Nationality?*"

"We've discussed it at length and it would be foolish
not to."

"Date of birth?"

"We're not planning to get married. It's for this reason we don't want to . . ."

"Address?"

"Perhaps with time . . ."

I sit down beside Lucinda to wait my turn and she encourages me:

"You have no reason to be nervous. Here these things are normal, not like it is in Mexico."

And in Mexico I wouldn't have the money to see a doctor.

"It's really good they don't charge here, right?"

She speaks to me of her daughters and of Hugo until the nurse tells me to go in. In front of me is a chubby lady doctor. In a friendly way she conducts me to the scales.

"Where do you come from?"

"Mexico."

"Oh, Mexico! Do you?"

Meanwhile she weighs and measures me.

"What's wrong with you?"

"Nothing."

"Then . . .

"I just want to take the pill."

"Oh, good for you!" she replies. Maybe she thought that I was pregnant.

A weight has been lifted from my shoulders; I'm surprised: so easy? I submit to an examination. Little by little my worries are erased; I look at the walls; I discover the diplomas and the accessories. She advises me of the risks involved and gives me a prescription. I am full of smiles for everyone. Before leaving, I see through the cracks in the blinds that the rain is beginning to fall.

10

In you are all the sites of recollection, the tunnels where
  the memory battles its entrapment,
the wingbeats of the crucified and the other side of the
  design,
the oblique truth of the soul and the boasting and the
  vacillation;
and you are the shore where the sea wounds its hands
  by contending with the land.

Someone knocks. Maybe it's Mr. Wolpert with the mail.
One moment! Ah yes, good morning. His name is
Andrew, Andrew Rogers. Pleased to meet you, yes. He
lives in the building, has looked for me several times, and
aunt told him that today he would find me at home. He
begs me to accept his invitation; it's not very far. "You
only have to see him to be convinced. *He's very proper* and
a very good sort, most definitely. A very good sort." Windsor is a charming little town and today is a splendid day to
see it. He has seen me many many times on entering the
building, and I have not noticed him with his new suit, his
elegant tie (100% *silk*), his well-combed chestnut hair, his
white skin, his large slender hands, although he is almost
six feet six inches tall. I think that perhaps the emaciated
aspect of José Carlos (why ultimately those dark circles
under his eyes?), his worn trousers, his dark skin, his way
of frowning, his beard, his long hair and rather short stat-
ure, are my idea of beauty.

Aunt hears the conversation and approaches us.

"Yes, why not. She has no plans today. She'd love to
go. You're very nice. The castle was exactly where we
were planning to go next week."

47

I sigh deeply, more deeply than ever. I need help; the job is open. I don't dare shout at my aunt to go to . . . there are no words left, and I think that the rain is an infectious myth. She has given me away! Bawd in ambush among the china and those deep chairs where no one can sit. It's true, yes. Mr. Rogers owns a car in which from time to time he can give her a lift to her office or leave her at Covent Garden, "please."

José Carlos, I bet you anything if you had a car . . . "that hairy person doesn't suit you, doesn't suit you." If she knew how beautifully you looked at me in the passages of the subway and how I enjoyed Hyde Park with you.

En route to Windsor I'm trying to think of a way of getting rid of Andrew; I don't know how to tell him or lead him to understand that I reject his friendship simply because *my aunt* accepts it. Well, the castle is well worth one less dispute between us. No, how horrible! I am being weak; I accept what is easiest, what I don't want, or seek, or desire. And how does she know if I have an engagement or not? Maybe I don't want to go anywhere that doesn't lead to the apartment of José Carlos. Ay, Mr. Rogers! Two things bother me: your way of driving, as though the wrong side were the right side—each time you make a turn I feel I'm going to crash against another Englishman as proper and hasty as you are—and what you may be thinking, because if it's about me you're on a road that leads nowhere. Lots of times it must be you I pass in the building without noticing it: that is the truth.

The tower of what century? Pardon me, I was distracted, a dream I had about going to bed the other day. No, no, it's of no particular kind. All this can be made very simple. Look, Windsor will be everything you wish, whatever you tell me. To inform myself, I'm going to buy one of those little books that are on sale everywhere for tourists, because now all I can hear is the noise of the coffee pot and the creaking of the floor. The guard's pompous uniform makes me think how ridiculous I must have looked to him in his pajama top; in the chains that we see I can still feel his arms . . . I remember my hair tangled around his neck, in his hands, on the pillow, everywhere . . .

11

Nights which were by some means verifiable,
nights that are not landscapes nor portraits nor
*   historical pictures,*
nights capable of being mentioned in the room where
*   love is made at whatever price between the point of*
*   departure and the critical temperature.*

My aunt has told me that's enough, that I better change
that bored look on my face, as well as my ill humor: "Wait,
wait. Soon they'll bring out the confetti, the streamers, the
assorted candies, the little candles," she says. "And all that
stuff," I say grudgingly. As if with that I might be able . . .
Ah! Now I understand! I will light the candies, eat the
streamers, and fling the burning candles.

Yes, the supper will be very savory, naturally, when it's
the wives of the bureaucrats who make it. If Lucinda prepared it, then I would eat it because what she cooks is
delicious. I hear what you're saying. I hear. They will serve
frijoles, *mole* Puebla-style, tamales, white rice; and there
will be tortillas, our beloved tortillas, very round and warm
and fresh from the *comal*. The trouble is that José Carlos
has convinced me of the absurdity of these parties; either
that or something odd, very odd, is happening to me. Why
my hostility to all these dishes that I like and which I
haven't eaten for months? Will the same thing happen to
me with other things in the future? "I told you you should
put on your dress from Campeche. Look, all the girls are
wearing their regional attire, and you ought to be like
them. Those beautiful blouses all embroidered by hand,
but you never appreciate the chance; you don't appreciate

anything. What's wrong! The party is going to be fun. Come, look alive!"

Why didn't you want to come, José Carlos? I'm beginning to realize everything you say is true: the forced faces, the chatter made up of clichés, the spiked punch, and all the commonplaces of the Mexican fiesta; clearly, if you were here, yes, if you who are a middle-class Mexican . . . but you're not that way, not at all what I am seeing. Now I can do nothing more than accept the fact that I'm seeing this and measuring it through you. I try to see everything as you would. I leave one lifestyle to enter into another, and it's difficult to leave one that doesn't work and take up yours, of which I'm not very sure. Shall I cling to it without opening my eyes? Is this what it means to be in love? A strange chaos that invades us and that satisfies . . .

I told you that Hugo and Lucinda would be here, but it didn't occur to me that this winter night they would come dressed in the garb of bureaucrats and spend the entire fiesta smiling at ladies with tremulous hands who sometimes carry the slender book *All You Must Know About Mexico* around in the subway, the same creatures who founded the club *Friends of Mexico* and who ask Hugo to come at tea time to give a little speech. It would be pushy to go up to where the two of them are, wouldn't it, José Carlos? Nevertheless, I would also like to go and interrogate him, not about Mexico, but about you. What does José Carlos think of me? Tell me, Hugo, does he talk to you about me? How's that? You, his friend who stays up with him until eight o'clock in the morning in your apartment living room, talking of everything. Tell me, yes, I want to know; it doesn't matter that afterwards José Carlos talks to me about the uncertainty and the insecurity and whatever else. I WANT TO KNOW. Why is he with me? Is it a game? Is there someone besides me? Many? Is he in love? Because I am, and maybe I'm just playing the fool . . .

What's that little raised floor for? Are they going to dance? Will a mariachi be among the things that have been ordered from Mexico for the fiesta? Sure, why not? If they have sent for ground corn meal, our dear tortillas, our dear chiles, hibiscus drink, tamarinds, tequila, sugar cane and crab apples for the punch, tortilla chips, earthen pots and . . . Also it's possible that among so many students who have arrived . . .—really, where did they all come from, since they never go to the embassy I know. I hope they're not going to turn Mexican; I mean in the worst sense and hope they enjoy "how great it is to eat a bite of *mole*, to see the oranges stuck with little tricolored flags made of rice paper which give that special Mexican flavor to our food, to the offerings to the dead, to Independence Day."

To your health! (Also it's true of the punch, José Carlos.) No, no, I haven't been sick. I don't feel ill. It's that I haven't been able to go . . . about the telephone you're right, a little call . . . but since I have been quite well and didn't wish to bother you, to waste your time. I always imagine you as so busy. Ay, many thanks, I do thank you truly; I promise you I'll go; you're very nice to worry about me. My studies? How are they? Well . . . I haven't studied much. Is Lower Cambridge very difficult? Yes, Mrs. Ambassador, I assure you that I'm going to study seriously, truly, you're right. Where do I go? To the movies, to school, to the museums, to the concerts, to the art shows, to school, to my apartment; yes, yes, to my apartment, to school, to the art shows, to concerts, to museums, to the theater, to movies, to the bathroom, and also, of course, I try to be a good girl and . . . Who do I go out with? Well, you see . . . uh . . . with . . . because . . . Ay, no! Please, no! Why do you want to introduce me? I beg you, it's not timidity; just between you and me I have a boy friend in Mexico. You say chatting never hurt anybody. But I prefer not to. Shall I tell you the truth? I've heard that he's very boring. Don't be offended; besides I don't like him; don't call him over; see, he's already going off to sing Christmas carols.

"Mrs. Ambassador, Sir Clifford wishes to ask you . . ."

Saved by the bell. José Carlos, what's happening to me is very serious: under other circumstances I'm sure I would have been able to have a good time. It's as though in spite of the fact you're not with me now, we're together, taking in the events of the evening, committing to memory each of the others' movements, seeing who it is that crosses the stage door entrance, mentally recording the voices of those who come here to forget the sequence of their empty gestures, to remember the Christmas parties which we experienced not so many years ago when we were children. But you're not here and who knows what you're up to, because I don't believe you're in your apartment. Let's see, let me think; now I know. In a rat trap theater in some far-off neighborhood you discovered one of those films "you ought to see, you mustn't miss," and you went there. What I'm afraid to verify is that you went alone. Where did you go? With whom?

A physics student chats with one of the guests and I listen:

"Don't tell me, smitten with Harrods? With Peter Jones?"

"And with the cashmere suits and the Scotch kilts and . . ."

"Let me inject a problem of elemental physics: How much force (expressed in foot pounds) do you need to lift your right arm thirty centimeters above your waist, bearing in mind that the arm weighs approximately (if I'm wrong, please correct me) three kilos seven hundred grams because of all sorts of bracelets and trinkets of pure 18 karat gold? Without taking into account any of these odd laws about

54

the dilation of solid bodies and the effect of temperature. I say this so you won't believe that the heat produced by alcohol will have any effect on our mathematics. Isn't that so, Miss?''

And I who thought that this type of problem would never be reduced to real-life terms. Look, my friends, I also have a problem: I don't know what José Carlos is doing. Let's see, according to the law of probabilities, where do you think he could possibly be?

Now it's time for one of the religious songs. They can't seem to agree on how to start. And the English who try to participate in the fiesta, what are they going to think of all this disorder?

"You should stand up and watch the children break the piñata. What rudeness! I don't know what interests you. Don't give me that sickly expression; go powder your nose. You see, they're gesturing to you to join them. What a beautiful rose! You who study anthropology, please explain to our neighbor just what a piñata is and don't tell me you don't know. That would be the limit.''

You see, Mrs. McDonald, a piñata, . . . *It's that beautiful thing you are looking at.* Only because you're the owner of the little dog I've taken a fancy to, I am going to tell you that it's both clay and jar, it's cutting up papers large and small, its glue, it's smearing, it's art and the result: little donkeys, stars, baskets, birds, dolls and that rose, the precious rose! And because you're *so very nice*, I'm going to tell you what they told me one day before I studied anthropology and I asked my professor, what is sin. And her position was: It's like the piñata, something that appears valuable from the outside, but it's necessary to break. Breaking a piñata makes a fiesta. Well, at least that's what she told me and I pass it on for what it's worth. And *I'm sorry*, Mrs. McDonald, because I don't remember what follows from the simile regarding the piñata's contents, and I agree to whatever your aunt, I mean my aunt, thinks in this respect.

If instead of the piñata it were that rose, I would be hung . . . No, no, what a thing to think! It's better that the piñata is for children; nobody denies that! Certainly, because they're children. Imagine, José Carlos, all these women who come from Mexico to buy trousseaus for their daughters or those persons who would completely tangle themselves in physics, all these young men, so strong, so drunk, and all the embassy secretaries who are so happy and not as serious or as bureaucratic as they appear behind their desks. Can you imagine all of them trying to break the piñata? People are right to say that one day in Paris at one of these little parties they threw a piano out of the window.

How nice, Lucinda! That after explaining to them what *mole is made out of*, that tortillas *are* like Hindu *chipati*, and what the tacos *are made out of*, you tell them to help themselves. Because even if I saw them seated and served plates of English propriety, I wouldn't have dared to suggest that they go there, even for the silverware. What would you have said to them, José Carlos? That when in Rome do as the Romans, and since here we're practically in Mexico they ought to push and throw elbows to reach the waiter? Then perhaps I might have helped by saying if possible avoid this false gentility; don't be frightened by the one at the rear, even if he gives the hardest shove and appears not to have eaten for years. Here you would have interrupted me: "The plates are served heaping, without leaving a bit of their surface visible." If I were an anthropologist, I would tell you that is the custom in Mexico because they always think it's their last meal, that tomorrow Gabriel will blow his golden horn. And of course they are not able to eat everything they took because, after all, it was not as good as it looked.

I'd like to know what you really think, José Carlos. Is it

true that you wouldn't have said a word to them? Look, Lucinda, tell them not to be afraid; *please, don't be,* for you're among the cream of Mexico: its best society, its artists who live six months here or in Paris, that we are the children of the bourgeoisie who have come to study; that the others, the students on scholarships, are not here.

José Carlos, is it raining out there? Yes, I realize I talk a lot about the rain, but everyone knows that here it rains almost all the time, and besides I like to talk about it. Therefore, José Carlos, I ask you while I'm watching this barbaric behavior which my grandmother wouldn't believe, is it raining out there? A question which, in short, I will answer tomorrow . . .

12

You are beginning to understand,
your love is sharing your bath salts, your religious
  holidays, your suppers with no one;
at times, the skeleton of your guardian angel dances in
  your eyes,
certain little wild birds wake trembling in your hands,
the vapor of the crucifixion
no longer makes you cover your child's nose "which
  knows nothing," "which understands nothing."

Christmastime.

"Mama, can you hear me?"

"Yes, yes. How are you? What's been going on?"

"I want a ticket to Mexico."

"What are you saying?"

"I'm coming back. I can't understand why I left home and everything's going wrong. I miss everyone more than you can imagine. I'm alone and with problems I can't solve. Mama, I don't want to be here. Mama."

If only I dared to take down the receiver to make that long distance . . . I could go on being a child for whom problems are solved. My mama would not deny me; I know that well, but being there I would lose José Carlos once and for all. I would have no part of him, his reasons for our living together despite his rough gestures, and everything would end that has to do with changing from a girl to a woman. It's hopeless. Why couldn't I have been the child of a washerwoman or some other unknown? Who would have believed this possible? At times like this my mother and her revolutionary forebears are nothing but

59

a burden. Yes, my general, although you might have been have-nothings until afterwards, now you're people of name and prestige. I regret that I never knew my father, who must have been everything that José Carlos reported having heard when he studied in Campeche. Who am I? What am I? What ought I to be? Now I know: the Greeks, the Elizabethan theater, etc., etc., etc.

In short, out of respect for Christmas, I feel myself obliged to write my mother the greatest string of lies, which I vomit word after word:

"Everything is going well. I have nine invitations for Christmas Eve: I will choose the best. I'll wear a blue dress and I'm going to ride in a black carriage which will meet me at the door. Although I'm far from you, I know I'll have a good time."

Really I should tell her:

"The distance between us is a measure of my absence. Without money, with my aunt and the problems that I have, I am sinking. At times I seem to be living in shadows and I wake up anguished as I did as a little girl. I know where salvation lies and I'm going to accept it. I am going to prove José Carlos wrong when he says I have no strength of character. I don't like to tell you this, but for me the Christmas celebration will be like any other. I have nothing to say or do. My aunt won't let me go out with the man I want to be with tonight. He's furious; I, filled with a desire to weep. And for this reason it's all the same where or how I spend Christmas. I hate all this that isn't mine: the house, the city, the friends, the parties. I hate Christmas because it makes me sad, and over and above that I'm beginning to hate myself."

On finishing the letter, I write "cheers" and the word emerges slowly, struck by the silence of the chill night air.

13

Where could I go to tell the truth?
What mask could I yank from my face to test the
anguish of my falsehood?
From what face could I pull my mask to test the fabric
of my life,
the great envelope that surrounds me?

It's almost five in the afternoon; this is the third time I've
looked at my watch. José Carlos has interrupted his work:
I don't hear the sound of his typewriter. I raise my eyes
from the book by Reyes he loaned me and find his eyes
on mine.

"I'm finished," he says, happily. "I'm going to send it
to my family as soon as I can. We'll see how they like it."

"It's awfully late, you know. It was for a good cause,
but I wouldn't mind something to eat."

"I'm about to die of hunger too."

As always, he's the one who cooks, while I bring a little
order to the room where he works, in order to turn it into
a sort of dining room. I go into the kitchen. How restful!
He is frying bits of meat, and I leave the restaurants and
the monotony of Steak and Kidney Pie, Stews, Yorkshire
Puddings, and Horse-radish behind. He speaks of Eliot as
if he just said goodbye to him; I wrap myself in an atmos-
phere of unspeakable happiness. Poor Marlo! To think that
there is always someone who loves us and we don't even
look his way, because that's life: disparity.

I am enchanted by José Carlos's thick moustache; his
long hair fits him well. I never tire of looking at him, of
hearing him; he always has some new expression and makes

me laugh. He finds things in me that until that moment I wasn't aware of.

"What are you thinking about so seriously?"

"You want to know?"

"Do you want me to know?"

"There's a fellow who's in love with me at school."

"Do you like him?"

"Does it make you jealous?"

"If I tell you no, will you believe me?"

"If I told you I don't like him and I wished it weren't true, would you believe me?"

"Tell me."

"His name is Marlo. He's my professor and it turns out that Cristina, my only friend at school, is in love with him. I've tried to help her in her romance. Imagine how bad I feel, José Carlos. There's no way I'm going to tell Cristina that it turns out he prefers me. It's really a problem, isn't it?"

"Is she Spanish?"

"Uh-huh."

"Good, introduce her to me and I'll make her forget him."

"Oh, you're very funny, aren't you?"

"Jealous?"

It's night already. Where has he hidden my purse? I can't convince him to turn it over. I tell him that no matter what he does, I'm not staying.

"Don't run away, coward."

"It's not that. We have been together all day. If you go on acting like a little boy, I'll have to go out and panhandle to buy my train ticket."

"Hypocrite!"

"José Carlos!"

"Who means more to you?"

"Don't torment me."

"You're afraid. Yes, afraid to live your life."

He hands over my purse and without saying anything goes into his bedroom, closing the door. I don't know what to do. Really I don't. I head toward the room and sit down by his side on the bed. I caress his hair without looking. I close my eyes. I tell myself it's only rain, wind, sleep.

Our bodies find each other again, cleave together in the night, are lost like the smoke in the chimneys.

14

Whose are these words now?
What movement do they cause in the conclusion of
  my acts?
What apparitions and what absences make them
  possible?

I have a fever. I try to decide what it is and I don't know.
No symptom whatsoever accompanies the temperature. I
die just thinking what it will be like to spend a whole day
in the company of my aunt, who must have returned from
mass. A lot of mass, yes.

I have promised José Carlos that I will look for work,
even as a nursemaid, and that with my first salary I will
move out of here. He says he loves me and will succeed
in making me move out. Therefore, because I know he
loves me, I have to do something quickly before he grows
bored and tells me to get lost. Tomorrow I'll ask among
my companions at school; there must be some job.

"Hi! You're the niece, aren't you?"

"Yes, come in. Who are you?"

"My name is Patricia. I work with your aunt and she
invited me here to eat."

"She's spoken to me about you occasionally. I don't
think she'll be very long. Sit down. Is there anything I can
get you? And since you already know her, I guess I don't
have to warn you."

"Of what?"

"In case she stands you up. What probably happened is
she forgot people were coming. She forgets everything
except making mincemeat out of me, I think."

Patricia is very well gotten-up. As if she had spent hours before the mirror trying to enlarge her green eyes and collecting her black hair at the back. I thought she was my aunt's age, but she appears to be in her thirties and is very attractive. Besides, with her short hair, French clothes, and her apparent nervousness she does seem younger. She's orderly, which I note just as I do that her accent is Guatemalan.

"Do you smoke? Oh, don't tell me they don't let you. And you're a fool if you pay any attention. Goodness, we get along well because I always tell her the truth. It's what she needs. How do you get along with her?"

"Didn't I tell you she was making mincemeat of my life?" I say, while lighting her cigarette.

"Listen, girl, you must be giving her gray hair by going out with an older man."

"Do you know of any work? Oh, excuse me. Don't use that ashtray; here everything is like in the shops: look, but don't touch. Let me bring you one from the kitchen."

"That woman makes me smile. She has introduced English boys to you and you don't go out with them . . . I tell her introduce them to me."

"But seriously, I can't recommend them to you. All they talk about is *How nice the weather is, isn't it?*"

"Then tell them to get lost and that's it."

"I wish it were that simple. I need a job to get out of this."

"Look, I share a floor with an Australian and an Englishwoman. Inside of two months the Australian leaves for her country. Perhaps . . . "

At last someone answered my SOS, and the possibilities of being near José Carlos increase. The only thing I haven't done, for everything turns out wrong with me, is to create an international incident between Guatemala and Mexico; I mean, *"you know,"* as the English say. Because with friends I have all the luck; when I was on the best terms with Cristina, Marlo happened to fall in love with me. The only good part is that I told her I was in love with José Carlos, and I've repeated it to the point of exhaustion. Thus Cristina knows it, but I feel guilty anyway.

"Patricia, do you know what you're offering me?"

"My friendship."

"It's mine in exchange for my aunt's, for you'll lose that forever."

"We'll do the whole thing without her knowing it, don't worry. She'll never come to my apartment. Now, chat with me. Who is that . . . ?"

I don't hear her finish. Already I see myself installed in a small room decorated with Victorian furnishings. I hear the Englishwoman preparing some tea and Patricia turning on the radio. I feel free, at peace, making decisions by myself about myself. I also see myself leaving the little room that was not Victorian, to go out with José Carlos. I like Patricia, who is open-minded. I'm entertained by her accent and can't avoid a smile when I hear her say "gurmonin" here and "gurnait" there. Our first encounter seems like something old, while being tomorrow's dawn. Roommate, I place all my tired loneliness in your hands, my friend, confidante and accomplice. I've been looking for you for a long time.

15

*The night falls like a great illegible book above the
   jungle.*

I feel so odd in Marlo's apartment . . . and it's because of
Cristina, whom I don't want to hurt. But it makes me
angry to fight with José Carlos, who says I'm trying to get
away from Charybdis, and I answer that I've started coming
to pieces against Scylla. And now my dilemma increases
because I don't know what manner of rock this is whose
name is Marlo, who is injecting himself in places where
he's not wanted.

As always, José Carlos presses, but I remain silent because
I want to give him a surprise; tomorrow they'll decide
about work at the school: teacher of Spanish. I'll move in
with Patricia and now I won't have to keep my seeing her
a secret from the termagant, whom finally I will tell I am
going to live my life. Then José Carlos will not have to
risk the rocks to see me, nor will we be faced with starving
together. On the other hand, if when he returns from his
trip he still wants us to live together, I will go with him.

Marlo's place is very small, and it's hard to endure the
cigarette smoke in my eyes; they burn. There are too many
of us for so poorly ventilated an enclosure. What a good
idea! On leaving the kitchen, glass in hand, a friend of
Marlo's uses adhesive tape to put our names on all our cups.
I don't know what Marlo is talking about with Jean, the
Belgian, who offers me a cigarette. How friendly!

"*Don't smoke it.*"

"*Why, Marlo?*"

Yes, it's very strong, but not a *Gitanes*. The two are

69

waiting for something, but I don't know what it is. Jean takes the butt away from me. José Carlos, what is this thing I am doing? What is going to happen to me? They want a reaction, but I don't know what. I lean against the wall. The smoke from Jean's cigarette drifts away; little by little, it scatters until it disappears. Each time the smoke leaves his mouth, it forms a sort of cone, plays with the air and is lost. It's delightful! Something that always happens and yet nevertheless I have never seen. I'm beginning to feel a prey to marvels. Imagine, José Carlos, if they knew I was enjoying this; what would they say in Mexico? She likes drugs and sex, is a fallen woman! I don't even know if I can tell you; all you'll do is squeeze me and serve me a glass of wine. Look, the colors have grown very intense. It's a picture in three dimensions; at the back, through a window, someone has painted a nighttime sky; I can't see the rooftop clotheslines: I'll never see them in London. Then there is a space occupied by the air that lets me feel its dense movement, and close up—very near me—are the others.

Cristina will be happy with Marlo, as I am with you. They move in a kind of slow motion. They follow the internal rhythm of their comings and goings. Everyone empties and then fills his glass again, but no *cubalibres* or *margaritas*, only wine: white and red.

I run into a pair of Belgian eyes; he speaks. I answer. We don't say anything concrete, but we understand each other very well. It's as if we were thinking, it doesn't matter what you say, I know what you mean. I understand until he has the stupid idea of inviting me to his home.

I order my body to move and go into the passageway. A candle throws my shadow on the wall, making it gigantic. I begin to dance to the music of Moustaki that wends its way from the diminutive living room. I watch the play of the sound with the shadows. I don't know what the others are talking about, but something must be happening.

We all laugh as though we've become simple-minded, and we laugh at everything. In a word, I am surrounded by a world of fantasy that is as real as I am, José Carlos. When I describe what I see for you, it will be a world turned topsy-turvy in which spirit has been converted into matter and values appear like deeds, in which, without ceasing to exist within, I am externalized.

I can play with everything — with words, gestures, rain . . . because it's raining.

I ask Marlo where the bathroom is so he won't follow me and go down the stairs toward the street. I walk. Tomorrow I'll know if they've accepted me for the job.

16

*The imagination is not always the best mirror in which
    to observe oneself,
in which to cross to the other shore
and at the same time be at the site where we're settled,
keeping a punctual appointment with our own gaze.*

"You must pay attention.'

"Yes, I'm sorry."

I don't know if I love José Carlos or not, or up to what
point I love him. And if I left all this to run off with him,
would I regret it later? And my mother: "My child would
never do such a thing."

"That's right, Christine!"

Cristina must be happy every time Marlo looks at her,
who in spite of her sweet and shameless flirting has not
been able to land him. Since she knows that now I give
classes and remain in the teachers' lounge, where I have
the right to enjoy the refreshment bar and take tea in his
company, she is constantly after me with questions: "Who
does he chat with and how much? Does he tell you if he
likes anyone? If I invite him to the party tomorrow, will
he come with me?" The only thing she hasn't asked me is
how many times he goes to the bathroom. On my word
of honor, Cristina, please don't believe I'm taking him
away from you; no, on the contrary, every chance I get I
drop a *She's very nice* or, by design, a *nice* about anything
yours or related to you. But you see he starts insisting on
helping me with something, on loaning me a book, on
paying for my tea . . . and I swear I spend my whole time
thinking about José Carlos, why I don't run off with him

since he gives me everything you want from Marlo. I believe that the guilt for all this lies with the nuns who taught us; they have infused us with their evil thoughts, their threats and fear of God. I would like to see them in my shoes. And if what's happening is that I doubt because I don't love him enough, even living with him, wouldn't I still have to listen to all those details about the "little middle-class girl"? Just because now I can endure being shut up with him in a room while he writes, can I be certain that all my life I could stand being confined in a lonely apartment, inventing chores while he pecks at his type-writer? Maybe then he would send me out into the street on any pretext so I wouldn't distract him.

"Alí, ask her if she . . . "

Why does he always ask Alí to speak to me? Is it because he knows I don't like that Algerian with his foolish face, find him even less endurable with his little song, "Si tu veux, c'est bien, si tu ne veux pas, tan pis, je n'en fairas pas une maladie"? Maybe José Carlos is insane and infecting me little by little with his craziness without my realizing it. He always treats me like a little girl. Perhaps he doesn't even love me, only thinks I need protection. Is he fooling me? He's too old for me. What is it he thinks? What's he doing now? He says that I'm very conventional, but I haven't noticed it. I'm the same as most, at least those I associate with.

"That's wrong, Luisa. Say it again."

Poor Luisa, she must be worse than I, in the hands of that dirty old man of an Arab who forces her to work while he makes out with whoever will let him. And now that they have charge of the little coffee break room, he'll keep her there behind the counter, serving the cups of tea and the appetizers, urging her to work rapidly, and then squan-der the money. José Carlos must think that I don't love him, that he doesn't matter to me, that I'm sleeping with someone else and that's why I don't go out with him. No, he'd never believe that of me, I'm sure. Why didn't he call me yesterday? Can he be going out with someone else? Lucinda is the only one who could tell me this, but I don't dare ask her for fear of what she might say. I couldn't bear to know that everything José Carlos says and what we do together he's sharing with someone else. I told him that I had to prepare exams for my students, that for this reason I couldn't go; that way if I show up unannounced at his apartment, I run the risk of hearing a woman's voice asking if she can serve him more coffee or if they are going out in the afternoon when he finishes his writing. And I can't imagine what I would do, because even if he goes with all the women in London I would still love him just the same.

"To wait, I wait, I'm waiting, I'll wait, I have to wait and I . . . "

That's it, waiting for him to call, speak, come to me. I wish blackboards in Mexico were like these, writing with a marker and erasing with water, not with chalk that gets into your very bones. But he hasn't even come to the school; is he getting bored with me? He must be happily preparing for his trip while I, the idiot, sit around thinking about him.

"If you dance tonight with me, you could . . . "

Once again Goffy with his dance; all he thinks about is dancing. That verb can be used as an example for all the others. They say that blacks carry the rhythm and the music inside themselves, but this one exaggerates, although he's certainly nice. How I wish to be with you at this moment, José Carlos, in another place, in another country. You say that you will remember me wherever you go, that you'll look for me in Paris, on the streets, in the mirrors, in the songs, in the places where men commune with their dreams, in the sound of the rain.

"Where are you, dear? Have you something to say?"

75

"No, I'm sorry."

I have to concentrate or Marlo is going to give me a lecture after class. What am I going to do when José Carlos is not here? I have begun to miss him and he hasn't even gone.

17

Dreams, that history without weapons,
that will that is part of the lips,
that pact with the heart that is briefer than madness.

"Since your arrival you've been very thoughtful. Something is bothering you, right?"

"No, Patricia."

"I think it must be having to carry your things away from your aunt's one at a time, surreptitiously. If it bothers you so much, there is still time to . . . "

"No, Patricia, it's not that. I'm counting the days until the Australian leaves and I can live here."

"I don't want you to think that I'm going to be like your aunt, but there's something bothering you and I'd like to know what it is."

"It's only a dream and I'm trying to make sense of it."

"Oh, good! That's nothing to worry about. I thought that it was a spat with José Carlos, some discussion with your aunt."

"Do you believe in dreams? This one must have some significance. I dreamed that I was walking toward Piccadilly at night. In the distance I saw something in the middle of the street; suddenly I realized it was a bed. Can you imagine a bed on the asphalt? It's not even believable."

"Would you care for tea?"

"Yes, please."

"And then?"

"Out of curiosity I went forward to touch it, and what do you think? It was my bed, the one in my aunt's apartment near the Louis XV chairs, the cut glass ashtrays, and the little porcelain figures which I believe dance every night. But if seeing the bed upset me, imagine how I felt when a policeman who had his back toward me turned around to face me. Do you know who it was? My mother."

"That kind of dream is enough to scare anybody; don't worry."

"A little more sugar, please. The worst thing is that day before yesterday I also dreamed of my bed, but a completely different and more horrible dream. I was asleep and very comfortable, but someone turned on the light and it made me so angry that I put on my glasses in order to see better, and I began to bite the blankets and tear the sheets. In total desperation I yanked the curlers from my hair: screaming. I went into a convulsion and with a pillow in my hands broke the room's furnishings . . . Horrified, I began to see what I was doing and ran to the bathroom to throw water on my face. What I saw had its hair on end, eyes sunken, and my thin nose was changed into a long snout. I had to accept it: I was a wild boar."

"Those aren't dreams, they're nightmares! We better talk about something else. Have you already told your mother you're going to live here?"

"I'm not going to tell her anything until a few days beforehand."

"And what does José Carlos say?"

"That I'll only be here while he travels and that afterwards we'll find a little apartment, where he wants to complete the book that he's almost finished. Hugo offered him a room, but José Carlos is not going to accept it, at least while he still has 'wool.' That's the reason I have to save as much as I can. Besides, I haven't told you that they're already offering me two groups more at the school. No wonder you looked puzzled! 'Wool' is the same as 'money.' "

"I think his trip is going to tell you how much you love him. That's good."

"How can I not love him when I've already decided to let everything go by the board to live with him? Rather it's he who will realize. I've told him that if when he returns he's seen that he doesn't love me . . . "

"Would he tell you that?"

"José Carlos, yes. Of course he would. But right now he's counting on my joining him and I don't know how because I haven't learned to rob banks."

"If I had money—how do you say it, wool?—I'd loan it to you."

"Thanks, Patricia. Don't you have a boy friend in Guatemala?"

"Many. But I never fell in love and that's the reason I decided, after having lived alone, to come to Europe. I never plan to return."

"Don't you like the Hollander?"

"I'm crazy about him, but he's so cold it's frustrating."

"I've got to go. I promised to meet José Carlos at five and I'm barely going to make it. See you tomorrow and thanks."

"I'll be seeing you."

I don't know why I worry so much about what I dream, when maybe I'm not even in London, nor do I know Patricia, nor have I ever been in love with José Carlos. What I should worry about is how I'm going to pass that lovely exam when I spend so little time in class.

18

Teeter-totter of the memory,
resulting mal de mer; *the present is now?*
The present is defined by the staircase of this dream;
to evoke a memory is to pluck a past desire.

"How did it go?"

"Very well. He was pleasant."

"What did he say about the manuscript you sent him?"

"That it marked a new direction in my poetry; I mean, there is a change in my latest poems. We spoke poet to poet, friend to friend, of Mexico, of painting, of the cuisine of our own southeast. When we realized it was suppertime, we went to a restaurant on King's Road, the three of us, and continued talking during the meal."

"His wife also spoke?"

"Yes, why?"

"Do you think that someday I could go with you and not appear ridiculous?"

"Why ridiculous?"

"I don't know what to say."

"I don't know much either. It's always necessary to learn. None of us knows very much. He's the exception; you'll see when you meet him."

"I met him in Paris. I was always much attracted by his personality. It was part of my world outside the boarding school . . . "

I can't be sincere with you, José Carlos, telling you under what circumstances I really met him. If I tell you the truth, you're not going to believe it or maybe it embarrasses me or maybe it sounds better to say: "I met him in Paris"

81

than to admit that my world outside the boarding school was not very large, that I saw many things without seeing them, that I heard much and didn't know from whom. You studied in Paris? What a marvel! Yes, within the four walls of the boarding school the bulk of the time, leaving the Eiffel Tower outside and the sleeping tramps under the bridges of the Seine, and later seeing Montmartre and Montparnasse from the car that carried me to the house of my mother's friends, who began receiving me on weekends, days off, and during short vacations. Ah, but the Place Pigalle, Le Moulin Rouge, and the Lido, not even from a car, gentlemen! And that was my world, apart from accompanying "my uncles" here and there on their visits to the Mexican Embassy, which naturally I made with them. Yes, that was where I often saw his blue eyes while I was chatting with Carmen, his secretary, while my uncles took care of business. It was there I spied on him through a crack in the doorway, seated behind his desk, pen in hand, with an open book, tapping his pen against the top, speaking to himself. No question that I saw his lips move and heard a gentle murmur issuing from them. One morning I accompanied my uncle to the embassy to see the consul. He greeted the *Maestro,* as you call him, and introduced me in the doorway. He was very friendly to me, said that he had known my father and had translated a book of his into French and written the preface. From that day forth something changed in me. Now I no longer spied on him because I liked his eyes or the calmness of his face, but because I began attributing characteristics to him that he certainly didn't imagine or would ever believe. For example, I stared at him and he would call me familiarly with his smooth voice, saying come. On entering his office I would see his hands; they weren't his, they were my father's. It was the same with his eyes, his mouth and everything else about him; it was my father doing this.

82

Carmen, who was my friend, would draw me out of these daydreams: "Your uncles are leaving now"; "They're looking for you so they can go." And the worst part is that in spite of all that imagining, I never found out who that gentleman was. I knew that he was a minister, intelligent, a poet, that everyone admired him. It was in Mexico, years later, when I was in preparatory school, that they mentioned him to me. And the same thing that happened with him happened with many others; no less than . . . Oh, now I remember. We are in an automobile on a wide boulevard; it's impossible to go forward quickly. What noise! How many horns are blowing! Two gentlemen have gotten out of their cars in front of us. They're arguing, shouting, waving their hands. Then they get back in their cars again and start driving with the same ferocity. Just as before, they hit their brakes and blow their horns. The crowd along the street is growing momentarily; I note that the majority are young people who come and go, bumping into each other as they cross the street. A couple walks beside the car, at the same speed. I observe them. Surprised, I discover that the woman, in spite of wearing eye shadow and lipstick, has no bosom, not even as much as I do, which is hardly anything. I look closely and her pants have a fly and her hands are those of a man. My "aunt," who has witnessed my confusion, speaks like someone who has been displeased: "Those fairies grow more shameless all the time!" I'm suddenly happy; I'm enchanted by the idea of seeing two flesh and blood homosexuals, of thinking that what I had imagined was true. Besides, to each his own, right? "We're going through Saint-Germain-des-Pres," she tells me. On turning the corner, we leave behind an old church and dozens of open-air cafes: Les Deux Magots, Flore, Sartre, Simone de Beauvoir. At last we stop in front of a kind of dead end like those you find in the heart of Mexico City. She tells the chauffeur to find a spot where he can

83

wait for us, and we go into a nearby building. I'm surprised that her friend lives in a place that's so old and ugly: Rue de la Grand Chaumiere. We go up a dark staircase to the second floor. I still think there's been a mistake. A blond woman of florid complexion lets us in; I note her height and elegant clothes. I think she's French, but her child's voice greets us in Spanish, in perfect Spanish. We can't sit down because she has just moved in and everything is out of order: cardboard boxes, books, pictures, clothes, clothes in every imaginable place. She apologizes for the mess, explaining that the apartment was a bargain, that it's very old. I see the thickness of the walls because she insists that they're the best part of the place and I don't understand, very definitely I understand nothing. Her daughter appears, older than I, and offers us a drink, including me, can you imagine?

"You, what do you take?"

The woman with the thin voice begins to talk about her struggle on behalf of the field workers in Morelos. I don't believe it's real; I am enchanted. I can't take my eyes off her, as though I were her accomplice. A boy comes in, of the type you see in Oaxaca; I don't know if he's an employee. I doubt it because of the way they treat him. Wrong again; she says he's an artist, a magnificent painter whom they've brought to Paris to study painting. Then I know I've reached my limit. I see the disorder as part of the decoration, as part of her personality. I begin to discover the little pockmarks on her face and they make me want to smoke. If I knew how to smoke, I would as she does. I am just getting into her world when my "aunt" says goodbye. I make a face that I don't want to go. They invite me to return whenever I want to, to join them in cleaning up, and I feel their sincerity; I believe them.

I pass two or three weeks wishing that my "aunt," good friend of my mother that she is, will go to visit them. Since nothing happens, I lie for the first time, but not the last: "My friend at school invited me. Let me. I'll be careful." I go out in search of adventure. There's something attractive about that place that demands attention, breeds enthusiasm, and I return several times. Always the same disorder, the clothes under and on top of the packing cases; but they have whitewashed the walls, the wood gleams, and the street can be seen through the windows. But we still sit on the floor. It enchants me to go because everything that's said is amusing, although I've never met the protagonists of the stories. Everything she tells me makes me laugh: "That little so-and-so of a Don Salvador; they had to give him a return ticket to Mexico the day after he arrived; you know why? He went up in one of those unstable glassed-in elevators which scared him so badly he went down by the stairs, asking for—what am I saying? demanding—his ticket. And that what's-his-name, your mother must know him, closed the Moulin Rouge last night; imagine everyone in hot pursuit of the show girls. These Mexicans are such a sad lot. That fine-appearing little fellow slapped that fool of a friend of mine after the cocktail party at the gallery. I would have sued him! But she's so self-effacing, such a goose, she's waiting to see when he'll do it again. I'm sure she enjoyed telling me all that because I listened with true interest, almost without blinking. For my part, I liked being recognized, just like an adult. My opinion mattered to her, and when her daughter said to her: "Why do you tell her these things?" she replied that I understood these things very well, that I was intelligent. What do you want me to say, José Carlos, that she also fed me *atole* with her finger? Sometimes she told me something about the Maestro; I thought they were friends, but never, not by the furthest stretch of the imagination, did I ever think they might have been man and wife.

"How's that?"

"Don't ask me. I have another reason for thinking I might be ridiculous. Imagine being in the dark a whole year . . . "

"I don't understand."

"Nothing, José Carlos, but with a little effort I can remember French." When I was in Paris with my friends, I saw the city so differently. I could remember it all, but felt it was a different city, what with their cleaning up . . .

"What's happening? Are we going to the movies? It's the sort of film . . . "

" . . . you ought not to miss," I imitate him.

How can I know that my words are true, José Carlos? I don't want to talk to you about Paris, where the vagueness of my actions reigned for a year, where night placed a veil over faces that I saw, where I was denied any knowledge of the truth because I was not prepared for it. But here, in this other city, where I can touch you, strip away the veil, where I have given you everything a woman can and want to learn to play the game; here, José Carlos, where I know it's going to rain tomorrow I can't pretend it's night, for I'm going to place my freedom at your table. I can't seek the four walls of my aunt's apartment and take refuge behind them. I'm here so I can see you. I know that you're the one that speaks to me; I know that yours are the words that surround me in the corridor of my consciousness. I realize that you are the one who is opening this other city to me, and I'm afraid, José Carlos. Fear of being a little girl, fear of losing you, of letting you go and later finding it may already be too late.

19

Tomorrow I will speak the word that dawns the following day, floating in the reservoirs.
Tomorrow I will speak the word that does battle at the banquets of the animals of winter.

Now it would do no good to tell Marlo to go back. I don't want to go. I don't know why it bothers me to tell him no. I thought that Richmond Park would be nearer. What weakness! At least Marlo is a decent sort; since I also give classes, he's gone out of his way to help, giving tips, constantly correcting my accent. Yes, yes: I was aware of that; that's true. Marlo is very handsome, but anyway I don't care for him, Cristina. Don't worry, I'm not going to take him away from you. I don't know why I told him I love London's parks, so green, so well cared-for . . . if only he hadn't gotten the car. How can I tell him after he went to all that trouble? Cristina, I swear to you I feel very bad about it. I give you my word I'm going to talk about you the whole time.

"Marlo, why don't you go to the University?"

Listen, don't tell me that you can't; you ought to do something for yourself. Almost everyone in the school is a student. Or are you going to give classes for the rest of your life? Don't thank me, I'm thinking of your own good. It's a pity that you waste your intelligence. In-tell-i-gence, ha, ha, don't laugh and correct me; it doesn't matter when we're on an outing. Look, it's more than a park, it looks like a forest. Is it very large? All the parks in England are like that. You're right. I like to walk. Are there always so few people? If only you knew . . . in Mexico we have a very large woods and every day is a fiesta there. You can do whatever you want, take the kids to the zoo; there they ride horseback or make little trips in carts pulled by goats . . . How did you say that's pronounced? They climb the trees, go on the swings, cry for cotton (it's like cotton but is made of sugar and is pink), also you can row just like you do here some places (mostly young people and couples; it must seem romantic to them, don't you think?). It's full of lovers everywhere, in the shadows of the trees, in the games at the fair. Yes, there is a very large fair. You see many grandparents taking a turn with their grandchildren and buying them almost anything to make them smile. True, there are many strolling salesmen: every kind of sweet, *tortas* (a sandwich, but with French bread), cheap toys, and even clothing. In the midst of all that hubbub you can always distinguish the whistle of the balloon salesman, who approaches from afar with a world of colors which float higher than a giraffe's head. You say there are deer? Ah, they wander around as though it were their own home. What? What do you want to know? In Mexico? It's different; nothing is the same. It's the family which causes all our problems. An example? Let's see, how many brothers and sisters do you have? One! Are you sure? I ask because with us there is always some doubt. I have four and that's small as the average goes. You're twenty-four? And you've been living alone since you were . . . nineteen? No, my brothers and sisters, known and unknown, live in their family homes twenty, thirty, forty years; often after they're married, and if they don't marry all the more reason. Yes, truly, my word of honor. Why would I try to fool you? Ask any other Mexican. What does your sister do? Oh, she studies at Oxford and has been living alone since she was eighteen. How nice! No, look, in my culture to live alone is to be a bad daughter, not to love the parents who give us everything. Why leave them if it's not for

88

some extraordinary reason? To study? Certainly, why not. Now more than formerly, but in spite of that the only thing we aim for is to marry and marry well; for if not, why should our parents go to all that effort to send us to the most expensive colleges? Career? Why, yes, many begin or finish one, but they don't think of it again. What's that? You're crazy. What makes you think our husbands would let us work? In my culture, no. All right. It is so difficult! I've already told you, it's obvious you've never known a Mexican co-ed before. I don't know how to explain this to you in English, but in Mexico the custom is that men do everything: work, support their wives and children, flirt, go on outings, lunch and dine away from home (for business reasons; don't believe it's anything more than this). I've already told you that in my culture . . . All right, Marlo, if you're not going to believe what I say, I'm not going to tell you anything. Me? They're already saying bad things about me at home because I go around in blue jeans, want to study odd things, and go out into the countryside to agitate because my school is insupportable. Those that go, I'm sure, are a little crazy; we feel good putting on local dress. We are a nest of little reds, you will say. Problems? Yes, the truth is I have exactly two hundred fifty-two prejudices, although at times I think I have only two hundred fifty-one. But, I say, right now if you want to know, I don't like your advances nor that insistence on taking me by the hand, although you hide it by clearing away a rock or picking up a switch. You're doing nothing more than looking for the proper hour and then *zaz!* She is made prisoner. Do I have a boy friend in Mexico? But why would I tell you? Now you're beginning to spoil the outing. That you like me? Ay, if you hadn't begun on that, I could almost swear I wouldn't have remembered José Carlos. I'm very sorry; if Cristina finds out . . . I can't help you. You thought that I liked you also? That I have flirted with you? That I have gone out of my way to be pleasant? I don't know why I should have done it, Marlo. To be perfectly frank, I will confess: I knew that the pretext for falling in love with me was this park with its deer, squirrels, and those beautiful birds; if José Carlos had seen them, he would have asked you their names. What are they called? José Carlos? Yes, he's a Mexican, is . . . yes, I care for him, I'm in love, I like him, he attracts me. It's horrible to suffer this way! Why? Because right now in front of you, I don't know if I love him that much, do you understand? Nor I, Marlo, and I'm not bothered by the fact you're holding my hand in yours. And now, what do I tell that silly Cristina? A kiss? Why, for what reason a kiss? Yes, he lives here, almost all the time. Okay, really not all the time; he's going on a trip . . . What? Why don't I live with him? Just one moment, it's not that I don't know the word in English. Wait a second, will you? I'm thinking. I can answer you easily. The words are right on the tip of my tongue, why I don't live with him, right? It's not fear. With all I've been saying I ought to be living at his side; I don't know why it is I can't, but something blocks me. Yes, he loves me. The same as you, he doesn't understand, thinks it should be easy. Tell me to go to the devil? Didn't you hear that he loves me? Listen, I am very complicated? Tears? Weeping? You don't have to understand it. I've already told you. Look, it's like a game: he pulls and I slacken; he slackens and my aunt and all the rest who surround us pull. How long (I sigh)? Tomorrow, and tomorrow I will say tomorrow and tomorrow the day after tomorrow (I smell a flower). Get married? No, in spite of what I told you before, we are not going to get married. I don't care, I know it, I can see that, I'll think about it. Why do you think I'm working (I'll put it in water when I get back)? Yes, tired of walking, let's go, all right? Listen, haven't you ever invited Cristina anywhere? *She's really nice* and I believe that she likes you. I'm really sorry to disillusion you, but I love him. He's part of me. When he returns from his trip, everything is going to change. It will be different; what with the money we have, we will be able to . . .

Since when am I kissing you? Now I do want to cry. I'm not sure what I feel, and I haven't tried to fool you either, Marlo. It's horrible. What's been happening? Already I don't know whether you are here with me or if I'm in this same country, at your side, or if the distance that unites me with José Carlos lies between us, separating us, you and me, stretching a bridge between him and me. Cristina, I am very bad, aren't I?

I can't erase the steps that unite me with you, José Carlos, nor retrace them. It isn't forgetfulness which has set my table; nevertheless, I was on the point of demanding a menu, of pretending that I was hungry, of seating my forgetfulness next to me and feeding it. We have kissed each other, and I'd do it again in the middle of this wood, without hiding my desire, without its surprising me, without trying to find the cause of this silence, without hiding my face, without suspecting that instinct turned the key, got into the automobile and came with us on an outing. What is this, José Carlos? The rain has begun to fall inside of us? Words that don't arrive? The wind that has played us a dirty trick? It was an absurd dialogue with the afternoon because I knew it wasn't your hair, that the rhythm of his respiration wasn't yours, and I couldn't find a single excuse.

Marlo, yes, let's go back right away; it's getting late. Don't ask me, but you know I must insist: I love him. Really? You want to help me? You'll see it's all quite useless. I would have liked to help Cristina, *you know. She's very nice.* And why haven't you realized yet that not only does she like you, she's in love with you and is my friend? I think a lot of her, she strikes me right, and I don't want the little fool to suffer because of me. I agreed to come because I wanted to break my ties with José Carlos. I'm a fool, aren't I? And I realize I love him more. I might have wished not to think of him and to tell Cristina that you spoke of her . . .

20

Thus everything has been completed,
and now in this place
we are disciples of this confused and millenary night,
of this atrocious music, of this city, of these words where
   it's necessary for me to leave you, and you me.

"Your health."

Surely he's getting up to say something, all that's been left unsaid during the meal, when the silence overpowered both of us, preventing us from making the least sound. He raises his glass. Please, say something, anything, *good morning, papers, afternoon* . . . something to help me bear up under the weight of your look . . . of my desire.

"When I come back, I'll take a room where I'll continue with my work. You'll come every day, read a little while pretending to study, but mostly you'll continue watching me. You'll die of hunger . . . we'll make love until finally one night when it has stopped raining, you'll decide to come with me."

"Your health," I say again. I pick up my glass, in the process stopping time, holding it suspended, as if everything came down to this moment.

As I wash and dry the plates I can't say anything: his leavetaking and mine. I, mute; José Carlos, odd, looking at everything as if wishing to learn it all by heart.

"What's the matter, José Carlos? You seem strange."

"It's my first experience with the Continent, travel nerves."

But no, it's not that. It's as if he foresees something . . .

"Do you know what I would have liked to be?"

"Yes. Actor, film director, poet, storyteller, painter, bull-fighter, novelist, architect, student, doctor."

There is a trace of a smile as he loosens my hair and looks at me tranquilly.

"Do you know what I would have liked you to be?"

I look at him fixedly; his answer makes me fearful, and meanwhile I shake my head.

"All the women with whom I've ever gone."

He suggests we move the furniture, "the way Hector had it when he left me the apartment, so it will be just the same when he returns." He remarks that he never was good at packing bags and asks me to help him. I go about folding his shirts and underwear and pajamas and my loneliness and my hopes and my illusions. I fit everything carefully into the leather trunk so that nothing will be damaged.

Words begin to flow gently in the warmth of the room; here our goodbyes are said. Someone changed the rules of the game, but I somehow didn't notice it. I ask him if he loves me; I don't like to invent, but I can read the answer in his eyes. He forces me to lie down beside him. The seriousness of the moment grips both of us. We know that time will judge us.

His body and soul search for my body and soul. Our debts settled by the afternoon, among the sheets, we are once again that man, that woman, in the rain, erased by the age-old act.

21

Understand me or don't understand me if you wish; I
*   am tired of your wanting to understand me.*
It fatigues me that you think everything can be
*   explained;*
the merciful air of your laboratories enrages me.
I didn't want to understand you, I wanted to be like you
*   because I feared you;*
because I conceded your correctness, I put truth in your
*   hands as if it were yours and I had to ask for it.*

"Dear Mama," I write, "it's been weeks since I've dropped you a line, and you must be wondering what's going on. No, no I haven't had much work, nor have I been sick, and the time that I study is relatively little; but I didn't know how to tell you what you're going to read. Oh, but don't be afraid; it's nothing serious. I've thought about it for sixty days and sixty nights and through all the minutes that lead from one day to the next; therefore, please don't think I've made this decision hastily. I'll tell you in the simplest words I can: I'm leaving the apartment of my fairy godmother (are you sure she attended my baptism?), to share a little place with a woman from Guatemala and an Englishwoman. Why? Because I've stood it until now. Yes, in all my letters to date I've always told you I was happy, that the fairy was just like the ones in stories, marvelous, and that I needed nothing to enjoy London and its rain, which each day grows a little heavier. Forgive me, Mommy, it was all a lie. At first because of your warning: 'She can be rather difficult.' Do you remember? I went on lying so as not to upset you. Since I've taken up lodgings with her, it's been very difficult, truly unbearable, and I would have left but for lack of money and the courage to confront you. You're fully aware that the money you send me is barely enough for transportation. That's the way you wanted it and I didn't complain. Now with the money I earn from my classes I can easily cover the rent for an apartment and for personal effects; and believe me, I'm a grown-up woman now and able to live alone. I'm leaving her because as a human being I should have done it months ago, because I'm tired of the moral blackmail to which I've been subjected since the first day and because only in the tranquility of my own room can I make the necessary decisions affecting my life. I don't want this to be a reason for displeasure on your part; don't worry, I'll be all right, to the point I think I may put on a little weight. I'm no longer a child and I've decided to go out on my own. I promise you that I'll continue going to the embassy to check in from time to time so that you'll have news, as well as proof, that I'm all right, Mama. If you want to break the spell, write the fairy and tell her that you know that I have moved and that you're in agreement, but above all that I should be left in peace.

"I say goodbye as always, sending you my love, greetings to my brothers and sisters; and I'm giving you the address where I think I'll be, at last, within a week and a half. By the time your answer arrives, I will be at the other location, there where the wind blows in the same direction, clearing the dust that swirls over this city and here won't let me breathe."

22

We can't go back, we can't return sliding
along that oil of ourselves.

If I closed my eyes, I could imagine I was in Chapultepec Park, running at six in the morning like any other good athlete, but I have to show what I have to Patricia; I want her to see it. Oops! *Sorry!* If I had remained there, waiting for the bus—it's been years since I've run like this—I would have told one of those maniacs who wait in line: "Look, sir, do you see what I have in my hand? It's a telegram. Yes, of course! You know about telegrams, but this is no ordinary one. It's from my mother. And do you know what she says? That she's sending me eight hundred dollars. You have it right, eight hun-dred dol-lars. No, no it's not for buying raincoats and umbrellas. Do you know what that money is for? Ah, I'll tell you at once. I must return to my country immediately. Yes, the one that's been in the news, host to the Olympics and world soccer. But do you know what it gives me the chance to do? Nothing less than to reach him in Italy, to make the voyage that I've been on some days, to give him a new reason for surprise, to bury my father dead these twenty years, not to go to mass on Sundays, to cry for my friends in the Move-ment of '68, to hear the birds, to enjoy music, to hate the noise of the traffic, to lose myself in the tumult of Picca-dilly, to buy that dress at Harrods, to catch up with him so that I can find myself." Afterwards that gentleman might have dropped out of line and headed for a pub on the docks to tell about the half-crazed foreigner who tried to sell him tickets to a world soccer match. The worst thing is I know the bus is going to pass me, and here I am running like mad. When I hear it approach, I will squeeze my eyes tight shut and will know that there goes the gentleman who saved himself from my discourse.

I almost lack the strength to climb the stairs. I'm totally winded. Patricia comes to see who's calling and is surprised to see me about to topple from the stairs.

"But what's happening to you, girl? You're panting like a dog."

"Read it, look what it says," I say, handing her the paper, which trembles in the air.

"And now what do you plan to do?"

"Go to Italy to join him and send the rest to the devil."

"Right now?"

"No, today I can't. I have to turn in my grades. Day after tomorrow, by plane."

"And your aunt?"

"I'm not telling her anything."

"And your mother?"

"I'll speak to her by telephone from Italy. It can't be helped. She'll have to accept my situation, and if she won't pardon me what the eyes cannot see, the heart cannot grieve . . ."

"But come in, come in a . . ."

"No, I'm going straight to the bank, to see if the money has arrived."

"So I'll have to start asking 'son-wan-to-chair-my-flat,' " she says to me in a mocking tone, and I see the happiness she feels for me.

23

A word, a history, halted in its waters like a boat
  that is going to be overhauled,
a story of love torn and later conveniently mended . . .

The window opens on sadness.
I lean my elbows on the past and, without looking, your
  absence steals into my breast and touches my heart.

Now nothing can stop me. With ticket in hand I go up to
collect the things I want to take, to fold the rest of my
clothes in order that *ma tante* (I'm so happy I'm speaking
in French) will have no suspicions when she returns from
her office and . . . But I don't know how much I can leave
because I've already taken almost everything to Patricia's
house. Well, in any case it's just as well since she'll probably
cause me problems by getting it into her head afterwards
not to let me take anything out of here. Come what may,
I know that nothing can obscure the happiness I feel at this
moment.

"*Good morning, miss. Have you forgotten something?*"
What do I tell him?
"*I have to take my clothes to the laundry.*"
"*You do look very happy this morning. We all like to see you
in that mood,*" he sighs, meanwhile ringing for the elevator.
"*Thank you, Mr. Wolpert.*"
I have been on the point of giving him a kiss and telling
him I am immensely happy. Mr. Wolpert, I am going to
miss you . . . I will pack my bags as quickly as possible, I
will put on the yellow dress he likes so much, and when
he sees me arrive he's not going to believe it. I'm not going

99

to braid my hair and it will make him happy to play with it, to tell me that it's like the night. Seated in one of those outdoor cafes, he'll tell me that at a sale in Spain he met an errant knight and some easy ladies. José Carlos, you should see how prettily it rains outside the window, hardly at all, as if the rain doesn't wish to block my plans; and it's spring! It's true, isn't it, we're a little alike? Afterwards we'll go hand in hand through the streets of that other city, and I will begin to silently imagine the approaching moment of being in the hotel room: your woman. We'll make love in a bed that isn't ours. After having slept for hours, you will open your eyes. You will place the sheet over my naked back and I will tell you that I'm not going to get dressed again, that I'm going to stay. Thus we will hide my desertion in a corner of silence and our bodies once again will be whirlpools: us, sleep, rain. We will speak of Mexico, of your sisters, of our dead: your mother and my father and how near they lived. You'll flash that easy smile; I'll praise your childish look; you'll dwell on your past aspirations, on your encounter with reality. You'll infect me with your liking for the Mexican poet Carlos Pellicer, your admiration for Lezama Lima; of Victor Hugo you'll say that he is great, your favorite expression. You'll open the window and start thinking again about my eyes and how I'm half woman and half girl. Later we'll go out to walk and then I'll tell you: "You know, José Carlos, I have decided to live with you. It doesn't matter that we don't get married; we'll live on your scholarship and my classes. I'm going to work and maybe later I'll also write. I'm free to love you and maybe one day we'll have a child as you have imagined, and it will know your city, your poems, your doubts and fears, your discovery of the world." José Carlos, to reach you I only have to take that plane.

On getting out of the elevator, I run into Mrs. McDonald, who always goes out for a walk with her little dog at this hour. Here the dogs have more privileges than our children.

"*Good morning, Mrs. McDonald,*" I say, and I whistle endearingly to the little bundle of fur which wags its tail contentedly.

"*Good morning, dear. Could I ask you a big favor again?*"

"*Of course, Mrs. McDonald.*"

"*We are not going to be in this afternoon. Could you take my little Spoon out, at six, you know . . .*"

"*Of course, Mrs. McDonald. Don't worry, just ask Mr. Wolpert to open the door and little Spoon will be out this afternoon.*"

"*Thank you, dear. Oh, thank you, dear!*"

No avoiding it, the poor little Spoony is going to urinate at six, not a moment before and not a moment afterwards, in the living room, in the kitchen, in the bedroom, and on all her things; and when Mrs. McDonald returns she will have every right to talk about the casualness of the Mexicans.

Good lord! All I need is the noise of the vacuum cleaner. It must be Esperanza, the servant from the embassy, a Galician who never stops chatting in her sibilant, lisping Continental Spanish. Esperanza, do you know how many times I've wished that instead of coming secretly from the embassy every two weeks to do the cleaning, you could come at least every other day? And not just because I'm too lazy to sweep and dust, but to hear you mumble about that little Virgin of Macarena whom you love so much and because you reminded me of my nanny who always was there when I was sad. But today, Esperanza, precisely on this day when I am so happy, I don't want to see you. If you only knew the things I am going through, José Carlos, while I see you writing, buttoning your coat, wrapping yourself in your red scarf, walking through the park, sitting down in the afternoon to talk about your doubts and fears. When I arrive you'll say: "You see how easy!" and you'll have no idea of my nerves, of my fear of being caught, of being weak. Now I will tell you of all the days that I tormented myself, saying: "I let him go by telling myself a thousand stories about how I didn't believe in the risk of the rain. For me, his goodbye was a road toward oblivion. I was afraid to lose myself in the shadows and to give my body to him silently, clandestinely, unconventionally" (as you would say). Now that I've told you all this, José Carlos, we're going to laugh, aren't we? Now the sadness is gone; I was never away from you and we ran with the water in the same direction.

Listen, Esperanza, I will act as if . . . I will try to be natural; the only bad thing is when they start looking for me she is going to say that she saw me fly the coop. Let's see how I'm going to divert you while I pack my bags, and then, how will I leave with my luggage? I'm going to tell you a story about how many dirty clothes I have and that it's easier to carry them to the laundry in a suitcase.

"Señorita, good morning! The last time I didn't see you. Isn't it unusual for you to be home so early from school?"

"Good morning, Esperanza. The reason is I have a lot of dirty clothes and . . . "

"It's been a long time since I've seen you at the embassy. You no longer remember your friends, and look, you're so well liked there."

"We're just on a different schedule, Esperanza."

"I'll be done with the noise in a minute."

I'll pack the newest thing I have first, my pink nightdress. *"You've made me so very happy; I'm so glad you came into my life,"* I feel like singing; and if this old woman lets something slip before my plane leaves? And if I ask her to go buy something while I throw everything into my suitcase, although it's completely scrambled, and if I put it in the little room for odds and ends next to the elevator? Esperanza, did you have to come today? That way, when

102

you come back I'll tell you I'm returning to school as if nothing has happened. Look, José Carlos . . .

"Esperanza, would you do me a little favor?"

"With pleasure, señorita."

"I have a headache. Could you go to the pharmacy for some aspirin for me? Pretty please?"

"Right away. I can imagine how you must feel after what I heard yesterday . . . And it appears that everything's in a muddle. Isn't that so?"

"What did you hear? What are you referring to?"

"Don't worry, I know that he wasn't on good terms with your aunt. You must be very sad; I won't say anything in front of her."

"What are you talking about, Esperanza? What do you mean?"

"What else but the accident your friend had?"

I drop what I have in my hands.

"Accident? What friend?"

"Don't you know? I'm going for your medicine," she replies, anxious to escape from my presence.

"Esperanza, please, stop being mysterious."

"First I'm going to run get your pills because I'll be late and they'll scold me at the embassy."

"Don't you see the state you've put me in?"

"Ay, señorita! Your friend the writer, that gentleman whom it appeared everyone liked so much; he suffered an accident."

"José Carlos?" I ask. "José Carlos Becerra?"

She comes toward me, nodding her head. Can she be fooling me? But where would this information have come from?

"Where is he? How is he?"

"Ay, señorita. They also said that the gentleman died instantly, in that city. I don't remember the name."

"It can't be. You misunderstood, Esperanza. Miss

103

Lucinda would already have told me. No one has told me anything!"

"Please don't tell your aunt that I told you. That young man—may God take him into his glory—has died. Everyone is talking sadly about it . . . The problem is to take his body to Mexico because . . . "

"José Carlos! José Carlos! JOSÉ CARLOS! José Carlos Becerra!"

"Señorita! Señorita!"

"Yes, Esperanza, I understand. José Carlos has died, hasn't he? He's dead. Now I understand . . . "

About the Author

Silvia Molina was born in Mexico City in 1946. She is the author of four novels and two short story collections, as well as a group of fables written especially for underprivileged children. A student of anthropology and recipient of a doctorate in literature from the University of Mexico, she has lived both in France (1961–1962) and in England (1969–1970). She now acts as a publisher in her own right, using the imprint *Corunda*.

About the Translators

John Mitchell and Ruth Mitchell de Aguilar are a father and daughter team whose most recent collaboration, *Qwert and the Wedding Gown* by Matías Montes Huidobro, was published in 1992. John is the winner of a Pushcart Prize for his collection *Alaska Stories* and Ruth a fulltime resident of Mexico for the last twenty-three years, where she runs a weaving shop in Pátzcuaro, Michoacán.